THE SKELETONS
STRIKE BACK

THE SKELETONS STRIKE BACK

AN UNOFFICIAL GAMER'S ADVENTURE BOOK FIVE

Winter Morgan

Sky Pony Press
New York

Sky Pony Press books may be purchased in bulk at special discounts for sales
promotion, corporate gifts, fund-raising, or educational purposes. Special
editions can also be created to specifications. For details, contact the Special
Sales Department, Sky Pony Press, 307 West 36th Street, 11th Floor,
New York, NY 10018 or info@skyhorsepublishing.com.

Sky Pony® is a registered trademark of Skyhorse Publishing, Inc.®,
a Delaware corporation.

Minecraft® is a registered trademark of Notch Development AB.
The Minecraft game is copyright © Mojang AB.

Visit our website at www.skyponypress.com.

10 9 8 7 6 5 4 3 2 1

Library of Congress Cataloging-in-Publication Data is available on file.

Cover photo by Megan Miller

Print ISBN: 978-1-63450-126-2
Ebook ISBN: 978-1-63450-127-9

Printed in Canada

TABLE OF CONTENTS

1
KEEP OFF THE GRASS

Steve returned to his wheat farm to find the fields were devastated. His vibrant farm, where his crops had once flourished, was now barren. A group of cows grazed peacefully on his property. Steve walked around inspecting the farm, searching for at least one carrot or potato he could harvest, but there was nothing but dirt. Somebody or something had destroyed all of his crops.

Henry looked at the cows chewing on the remaining few pieces of wheat. "Those cows must have spawned while you were away, Steve," he said.

"It also looks like a few creepers exploded on the wheat," Lucy commented as she looked down at the burnt patch of lawn.

"You need to build a fence," Max suggested.

Steve had been away from home helping save his treasure hunter friends, Henry, Max, and Lucy, who were trapped in a desert temple by evil rainbow griefers, and had just returned to the farm with his friends. His ocelots, Snuggles and Jasmine, and his dog, Rufus, greeted him. But Steve was too distracted for a proper reunion.

Lucy noticed Steve was upset and reassured him. "We can help you build the fence. I have some ideas that might keep the animals off your lawn."

"Without the wheat and my other crops, I don't have any resources left to trade. And after our adventure, my inventory is very low. How am I going to replenish it?" asked Steve.

"We can trade the treasures that we found in the desert temple," continued Max as he opened a chest and pulled out a few diamonds.

"Diamonds are very valuable. They can get us a lot more than a bunch of wheat, carrots, and potatoes could get us." Lucy looked through the chest and held emeralds in her hand.

Henry had a different suggestion. "Yes, we can trade our diamonds, but if we find a creeper and we get it to blow up a tree, we can get some wood to build the fence without having to give up any of our treasure."

"That's a fantastic idea," said Max, "but I don't think we will have enough wood."

"So, when we get the creeper to blow up a tree we'll use the wood from that tree to make axes, and then we can cut down trees and build a bigger and stronger fence," Henry told them.

"But where are we going to find a creeper?" asked Lucy.

It was still daylight and creepers only came out at night.

"There were so many times when I was terrified because I saw a creeper and now we actually want to summon one?" Steve told them. He wasn't sure about Henry's idea.

As the group talked, another cow ambled onto Steve's farm and began to trample the little patch of grass that was left. The cow leaned down and ate the last bit of wheat.

"We have to do something soon," Lucy said, "or you won't have a wheat farm left."

Steve looked through his inventory in search of wooden blocks, but the inventory was bare. Steve kept searching as the sun began to set.

"Great! Dusk! This is the perfect time to find a creeper." Henry was very excited to go on a creeper hunt.

Steve could see a creeper off in the distance, but was hesitant about pointing it out to the group. His friend did not have the same reluctance.

"A creeper!" Lucy called out.

"We need to lead it to a tree," exclaimed Max.

The group put on their armor and sprinted toward the green blocky creeper.

"Keep Snuggles and Jasmine away. Ocelots scare them!" Lucy informed the group as they closed in on this hostile, fiery mob.

Steve held his diamond sword tightly, as he kept a lookout for other hostile mobs that might be lurking in the darkness.

Henry and Max charged toward the creeper, herding it toward some trees.

Max took out his bow and arrow and aimed for the black-eyed mob.

Tick. Tick. Tick. Boom!

The creeper exploded, destroying a nearby tree.

Max walked toward the charred tree and picked up the logs. "I think we can make at least two axes from this wood."

"Do you guys spot any other creepers?" asked Lucy.

Max placed a torch, using the light to search for creepers in the distance. "No, I don't see anything at all."

"Watch out!" Henry screamed to the group. "Zombies!"

A group of green-eyed zombies slowly walked toward the entrance to Steve's house.

"Oh no!" Steve cried out, "They are ripping my door off the hinges!"

A zombie banged the door until it fell, as two other zombies followed him into Steve's house.

"It looks like we're going to need more wood," said Max.

"No way, I'm building an iron door next time. I only used wood because we didn't have many resources after Thomas destroyed my house! We have to stop those zombies!" Steve hastened toward his home.

"This is what happens when you go out at night," said Lucy as she followed closely behind Steve.

"It wasn't my idea," Steve defended himself.

The group could see the zombies walking through Steve's house. They were searching for victims, but the house was empty.

The zombies walked out of the house. Max shot an arrow at one, striking it. The zombie was hit, but still alive. Steve barreled at the zombies with his diamond sword and hit the weakened zombie and destroyed it.

Lucy, Henry, and Max took out their diamond swords and began to battle the zombies.

Henry whacked a zombie with his sword. Max and Lucy cornered another zombie and destroyed it with their swords. The zombie attack was over.

"How are we going to sleep in a house without a door?" asked Steve as he walked through his house, inspecting the damage the living dead creatures caused to his beloved home.

"It looks like the only serious damage they caused was to your door," Lucy remarked, looking around Steve's living room. His walls were adorned with emerald designs.

"That's a huge problem," said Steve. "Look at what's crawling past the door right now."

The group turned to see four pairs of red eyes staring at them from the doorway.

"Spiders!" Henry raced out the door and struck the first spider with great force, instantly clobbering the arachnid.

Max, Lucy, and Steve hit the spiders with their swords.

"It's going to be a long night," Steve remarked, as he picked up the spider eyes that dropped on the ground.

"Great, spider eyes," said Lucy, "we can use these for brewing potions."

Henry stood by the door and watched for hostile mobs. "Don't worry," he told them, "it's almost dawn and soon the hostile mobs will be gone."

Steve was tired, but he knew it was too late to get more than a little sleep. "You're right," Steve said, "maybe that's the last of the hostile mobs."

Max lit a torch and placed it on Steve's wall, as the gang looked out the window, ready to pounce on any hostile mobs that approached the house.

"It looks like the night is calm," Henry said. "Maybe we should try to get some sleep. If you guys want, I can keep watch at the door until morning. I'm not that tired."

Steve was relieved. He was exhausted. "Thanks," he said gratefully, and looked at Henry with tired eyes.

As Steve, Lucy, and Max made their way toward their beds, a voice cried from the distance.

"Help me!" the familiar voice called out.

"Oh no! That's Kyra!" Lucy said, and the group hustled to Kyra's house.

2
FENCES MAKE GOOD NEIGHBORS

The group raced to help Kyra. When they reached her house, Kyra was dressed in armor and in the middle of an intense battle with two spider jockeys.

"Two spider jockeys! I didn't even know that could happen." Henry was worried about Kyra, but also impressed by this rare find.

Kyra had been struck by the skeleton's arrow and was barely able to lift her sword as the skeleton riding a spider lunged toward her.

The spider was inches from Kyra's arm when Steve struck the arachnid with his diamond sword. Max shot an arrow at the skeleton, obliterating it. Henry and Lucy fought the other spider jockey. Lucy tried to strike the skeleton with her diamond sword while avoiding the sea of arrows the skeleton flung in her direction. Henry hit the spider with his diamond sword, weakening the creature until it was destroyed.

"Kyra, are you okay?" Steve asked his friend. She tried to sprint toward her house, but she couldn't. Her hunger bar was incredibly low.

"Drink this," Lucy said, handing Kyra a potion of healing. "It will make you feel so much better."

Kyra drank the potion and began to feel stronger. "Thanks, guys. I can't believe I was attacked by two spider jockeys."

"I know. That's incredible," remarked Henry.

"I was trying to go to bed, but I couldn't because there was a warning that a hostile mob was nearby. I put on my armor and assumed it was just a zombie or a creeper, but when I walked outside there were two spider jockeys outside my door. If you guys hadn't showed up, I don't know what would have happened." Kyra was so glad she had a neighbor like Steve; he was always there when she was in a bind. She knew she could count on him.

"We were also battling hostile mobs." Lucy told Kyra about the spiders, zombies, and the creeper that destroyed a tree.

"But we wanted the creeper to destroy the tree because we needed wood. We are building a big fence around my property," said Steve.

"Why? Are you trying to keep your neighbors off your property?" asked Kyra.

"No, I'm trying to stop cows and creepers from destroying my crops. I always want you to come over to visit!" Steve told Kyra.

"Once we finish the large wooden fence, we should put a carpet on top of it. People can jump over the carpet, but hostile mobs can't," said Lucy.

"Yes, placing a carpet on top of the fence is much better than leaving a gate in the fence open," added Steve.

"Speaking of gates and doors, a zombie ripped Steve's door off its hinges. We have to fix it now," Max said as the sun rose behind him.

"Finally! It's dawn! We're safe." Lucy was excited. She offered to hunt for a chicken to roast for the group. "Since we didn't get any sleep, we should really eat something so we have enough energy to build the fence."

"And rebuild the door," said Max.

Lucy looked out at the green pasture and searched for chickens. She found a few and began to prepare the morning feast.

Meanwhile, the others had returned to Steve's farm and were at work breaking down trees and making wooden planks for the fence. They took a break to eat the roasted chickens.

"I think we can finish this fence by the end of the day," Henry said, staring at the wood in his inventory.

"Let's not forget about the door," Lucy said and took a bite of chicken.

The gang used wooden planks and sticks to build the fence. Working together made the job go by a lot faster than they expected. The group felt confident that the fence was high enough to protect the crops from hostile mobs and animals. Snuggles, Jasmine, and Rufus sat by and looked on as the group built the fence. Steve turned around when he heard Snuggles meowing.

"Someone is approaching," Steve told them. "Snuggles only meows when strangers are approaching."

Henry and Max took out their diamond swords.

"It could be a griefer," Henry said as he looked for a stranger in the distance.

"Are you sure Snuggles only meows when strangers are near?" Lucy questioned. She wanted to finish the fence and rebuild the door without any distractions.

"Look!" Max said as he spotted someone walking in the distance.

"It's not a stranger!" Kyra was excited.

"It's Georgia!" Lucy rushed toward their old friend.

Georgia walked onto the wheat farm. The gang hadn't seen her since the building competition on Mushroom Island.

"Georgia, why are you here?" asked Steve.

Georgia was excited to see her friends, but was visibly exhausted. Her hunger bar was very low. Lucy offered her some chicken.

"This has been such a long trip. I thought I'd never get here." Georgia could barely get out the words, but she ate the chicken and began to feel better.

"Where do you live?" asked Henry.

"I live in a village very far from here. It's past the Mesa Biome and the Flower Forest," she replied.

"That's very far," Steve remarked. He had heard of the famed Flower Forest and its gorgeous tulips, but had never traveled there.

"I had to come. You were the only people who could help us," said Georgia.

"Us?" asked Steve.

"My village. It's being destroyed. You're our only hope for survival." Georgia looked at the gang. "You did such a great job saving the building competition. You're the best warriors I've ever encountered."

Steve couldn't believe Georgia referred to them as *warriors*. He looked at his friends. He knew they had to help Georgia and her village.

"We will help you!" Steve replied.

"What happened to your village?" asked Lucy.

Georgia began to speak, but stopped and burst into tears.

3
THE STORY OF THE SKELETONS

Georgia told the group about her village. "Every evening an army of skeletons rushes through the village to attack us. It's destroying my quiet village. My friends and I spend all of our time securing our streets from an attack, but it doesn't seem to help."

"That's awful," said Lucy.

Steve sprinted toward his chest, opened it up, and took out his armor and diamond sword. He put the armor on and raced back to the group. "We must save Georgia's village. Let's get ready!"

The gang followed Steve and filled up their inventory with the necessary items for battle and their long trip to Georgia's village.

As they gathered their final supplies, night began to set in. "We can't travel now," Steve told the group. "We'll waste all of our energy. We have to wait."

Lucy spotted a creeper in the distance and took out her bow and arrow.

Kaboom!

"We need to get in our beds," said Kyra.

"But I don't have a door," Steve said, looking at his house. When Georgia arrived they had abandoned all of their rebuilding projects.

"Let's go to my house," suggested Kyra.

The group hurried toward Kyra's house. Kyra's front door was in sight, but two Endermen stood by the door. They held blocks as their purple eyes glowed in the night sky.

"Don't look at them," Steve reminded the group.

It was too late. Henry accidentally made eye contact with one of the Endermen and it opened its mouth, readying itself for an attack. Henry took out his diamond sword while the Enderman shrieked and teleported toward him.

"Lead him to the water!" Steve called out to Henry.

Henry ran toward the village's shoreline. He could hear the high-pitched sound from the Enderman growing louder. He sprinted as fast as he could, but the Enderman's sounds were deafening. The shore was still too far away and he couldn't plunge into the safety of the water. Henry turned around and struck the Enderman with his diamond sword. The sword landed on the Enderman's chest, but didn't destroy the powerful mob. Henry struck the Enderman again. The Enderman shook and then struck Henry. Max rushed over to Henry with a bucket of water, and he threw it on the Enderman, destroying the dark, lanky creature.

"Thanks, Max. What happened to the other Enderman?" asked Henry.

"Kyra threw a bucket of water on him," Max told his friends as they walked toward Kyra's house.

As Henry approached the house, he couldn't find any of his friends. "Where is everybody?"

"They went to bed. And we have to get to bed before we start our trip to Georgia's village," Max told him.

Steve ran out of Kyra's house and called out, "Look out guys! Zombies!"

Max and Henry took out their diamond swords, ready to battle the zombies. But there were too many to fight.

"Get the others!" Henry called out to Steve.

Max skillfully battled three zombies, but even this zombie invasion was too much for the master swordsman.

Kyra, Lucy, and Georgia joined in the battle, lunging toward the zombies with their swords.

Georgia only had a wooden sword. "My diamond sword was stolen by a griefer on my trip here."

"That's awful," said Lucy as she struck a zombie with her powerful diamond sword. "We will help make you a new diamond sword and enchant it. You'll need it for the journey back to the village."

There were three zombies remaining. Max took out his bow and arrow and with perfect aim shot three arrows that struck and destroyed each zombie. Henry watched in awe.

"Wow, Max, you are a master fighter!" Henry said with a smile.

"I'm glad you're coming with us on the journey to my town. I don't think we'd be able to defeat the skeletons without you," added Georgia.

Steve listened to all his friends congratulate Max. Although Steve knew Max was a skilled fighter, he was worried that skeletons would outnumber them. Steve knew they had to help Georgia, but he hoped this wasn't a fool's errand.

Georgia noticed Steve's pensive expression and said, "Steve, I can tell you're worried about our trip."

"I am. I worry that we'll disappoint you and your village. What if we can't save your homes?" Steve paced around Kyra's house as he spoke.

"You're right," said Lucy. "Maybe we can't save Georgia's village from these evil skeletons, but if we don't try, we'll never know. Also you can't give up on a friend when he or she comes to you for help."

Steve knew Lucy was right. "I know, but we have to be prepared and we must have a plan."

"I think the first item on our agenda is making Georgia a diamond sword," Max said, and he opened up his chest and gave Georgia two diamonds. "Take these and I'll help you craft a powerful enchanted sword."

Georgia was shocked. She didn't know how to thank Max for his generosity. Diamonds were an incredibly rare find and to give them up without asking to trade anything was an extremely kind gesture.

Steve took out his crafting table and they began to work on Georgia's sword.

"We can use this enchantment book," offered Lucy as she took out a book from her chest and started to enchant the sword with Kyra's anvil.

Georgia held her sword and waved it in the air. "This is fantastic. It's even more powerful than my old sword. Thanks, guys!"

The group gathered the rest of the supplies for their journey to Georgia's village.

A spider crept past Kyra's house. Georgia ran out and clobbered it with one hit from the new sword.

"I've never been so excited for nighttime," exclaimed Georgia.

"Don't get too excited. We should go to bed. We need to rest for the journey," said Steve.

They were finally able to sleep. There were no hostile mobs lurking around the house. Steve walked toward the comfy bed in Kyra's house. His heart was beating very fast as he thought about tomorrow's adventure. Steve imagined how scared the people in Georgia's village must be each night. He couldn't imagine his friends Eliot the Blacksmith and Avery the Librarian surviving a nightly battle and living in a town that was constantly attacked by skeletons. Steve took a deep breath, knowing he had to be strong and he had to help these villagers, as he drifted off to sleep.

4
JOURNEY TO THE VILLAGE

The sun was shining and the gang was ready to embark on their journey. As they left Kyra's house and walked past Steve's wheat farm, they noticed something was missing.

"Steve!" Lucy cried out. "We never made your door!"

Henry grabbed iron ingots from his inventory and quickly began to build a door for Steve.

"I know if we let you design the door, we'll have to wait all day. You are a perfectionist when you build," Henry joked. The others joined him in building the door. They tried to finish the project as fast as they could because they needed to start their trip.

Henry placed the door on the hinges. "What do you think?"

Steve stared at the iron door on his stone house. "It looks great. Now every time I enter my house, I'll think of you guys."

"Great!" exclaimed Lucy. "Let's hurry to Georgia's village. We have some skeletons to battle."

The group walked through the green pastures past Steve's local village, making their way to the swampland outside of the town.

"I hate the swamp biome," Kyra remarked as she walked past oak trees covered with vines.

"Why?" asked Georgia.

Kyra walked along the shore, looking at the lily pads floating in the murky water. "There's something really creepy about the swamp. And I'm afraid of slimes."

"We don't have to worry about slimes; it's still light out," said Henry.

"But we do have to worry about witches," Max said, pointing at a witch hut a few feet in front of them.

"Oh no!" Lucy called out.

"Don't worry," said Max, "it might be empty."

A bat flew overhead. The sun began to set.

"We have to spend the night in the swamp." Kyra's voice quavered. She was terrified.

"Can we construct a house quickly?" asked Georgia. She didn't like the swamp either and wanted to find a way to shelter them from a night out in the open.

"I don't think we have time!" Steve shouted as a witch with white vacant eyes and dressed in a purple robe emerged from her hut. The witch clutched a bottle of potion.

"What should we do?" cried Georgia.

Max grabbed his bow and arrow and aimed toward the evil witch, but the arrow struck her black hat and missed her body.

"Try again!" Georgia called out.

Max shot another arrow, and this one struck the witch in the stomach, but made no impact. The witch drank a potion and grew stronger and faster. She zoomed toward the group.

Georgia took out her new powerful diamond sword and charged toward the witch.

"Take this!" Georgia said as she struck the witch.

The witch splashed a potion on Georgia and she began to feel incredibly tired. "What has she done to me?" Georgia asked as her body lost all energy.

Max shot another arrow at the witch and it hit her leg.

"Good job, Max. The witch is getting weaker," Henry said, and hit the witch with a powerful blow from his diamond sword.

Lucy ran over to Georgia and gave her some milk. "You'll feel better soon. She just splashed a potion of poison on you, but milk will help you recover," Lucy reassured her friend.

The witch took another drink from her bottle and grew even stronger. She sprinted toward Kyra and Max. They tried to fight back, but it was too late. She splashed a potion of poison on both of them.

Lucy and Steve took out their diamond swords and, with all of their might, they clobbered the creepy evil witch. The witch dropped a glass bottle and a spider eye. Steve picked them up, as Lucy rushed to her friends and gave them milk.

"How are we going to get through the night?" asked Kyra. "I can barely move."

Georgia walked over to Kyra and Max. "The milk really helps. I couldn't even move at all, and now I feel fine."

A bat flew very close to Steve's head. "Is that a sign that another witch will be here soon?"

"I hope not," Max mumbled, for he could barely get the words out as he drank the milk.

The bat flew past the full moon. The group stood and thought of their next move while trying to recover from the witch attack.

"What's that sound?" Lucy asked.

"I don't hear anything," replied Henry.

"Shh!" said Lucy. "Listen."

The gang was very quiet. "Can't you hear it?" asked Lucy again.

Plop! Plop! Bounce! There was a faint sound coming from a nearby cave.

"Sounds like slimes!" Henry called out. "Is everybody ready? We need to attack the slimes before they come after us."

"Not slimes!" Kyra was terrified.

"It's too late!" Max pointed at four slimes bouncing toward the group. The sound of the gelatinous creatures was growing louder as the medium-size slimes bounced toward the group ready to attack.

Georgia struck a slime with her diamond sword. The slime broke into two smaller slimes. "Help!" she called out. Max used his remaining bit of strength to crush the two smaller slimes.

Three green cubes jumped at Kyra. She fought back, but she needed help. The gang joined Kyra in a battle against the gooey green beasts.

Every time they hit the bouncy creatures, it created even more slimes. "This is never ending!" Henry cried out as a sea of small slimes hopped around the group.

Steve was struck by one of the slimes, and his health bar was diminished. He hit a slime, but it jumped up high in the air and pounced on him.

"We need to help Steve!" Lucy said as she battled her own slime enemy. "If we don't, he's going to be killed!"

Two slimes cornered Steve and were pouncing at him. He didn't have enough energy to strike them with the diamond sword. He was fading. Steve needed help fast.

Lucy destroyed the slimes that attacked her and rushed to her friend's side, but a slime jumped on her. Henry and Kyra joined Steve and battled the slimes. They destroyed them. The slimes were gone.

"Do you hear any more slimes?" Steve asked weakly.

His friends stood by his side. They gave him a potion of healing and watched him take sips from the bottle, hoping it would work.

5
GOOD GRIEF

Steve drank the potion and grew stronger. The sun began to rise as the group continued on their journey to Georgia's village.

The swamp biome turned into a mountainous biome, and they used all of their energy to trek up an enormous mountain covered with snow. As they stood on the mountain's peak, Georgia looked off in the distance. "I think I can see my village. It's not that much farther."

"Everything seems smaller from up here," Henry warned her. "Don't get too excited, we still have a way to go."

The gang made their way down the mountain and into a forest. "Let's not get lost here," remarked Steve. "There are a lot of leaves and it's hard to see where we are going."

They walked slowly through the leafy path, until they stumbled upon a jungle temple. The grand temple was located on a small river. Trees shaded a large portion of the temple.

"Wow!" Lucy called out, "Treasure!"

"Didn't we find enough treasure on our last trip?" asked Steve, and then he reminded her why they were on this journey. "We need to save Georgia's village. It's almost nightfall and they are probably already scared they will be attacked tonight. We have to think of them."

"I guess you're right," replied Lucy.

The group planned to pass up a trip to the jungle temple until Max said in a loud whisper, "Look, it's a rainbow griefer!"

The rainbow griefer stood in front of the jungle temple and seemed to be threatening two innocent people dressed in leather armor.

"Their armor isn't even strong enough to protect them," Henry said as he stared at the two people.

The rainbow griefer took out his sword and swung at the two victims. Max couldn't just stand back and watch the griefers terrorize innocent people, so he took out his bow and arrow and aimed at the rainbow griefer. The arrow shot across the grassy path and hit the griefer in the chest.

The rainbow griefer was infuriated. He looked out at the forest trying to find the person who attacked him.

The two leather-clad people used the opportunity to strike the griefer with their wooden swords. The griefer tried to fight back, but Max shot another arrow and it struck the griefer in the arm.

"Let's go!" shouted Max as he led the group toward the rainbow griefer.

The gang took out their swords and surrounded the griefer, striking him until he was destroyed.

"Thanks! You saved us. I'm Sophie, and this is my friend, Tatiana." She smiled and asked, "How can we repay you?"

The group introduced themselves, and Max said, "You don't need to repay us. We couldn't walk by and watch a rainbow griefer attack you. We've dealt with rainbow griefers before, and they are vicious."

"I had never seen one before. I was thinking it was so colorful and pretty when it spotted me and began to attack," said Sophie.

"I don't think it's alone," warned Tatiana. "I'm pretty sure there are other griefers in the temple."

Steve wondered if they should go into the temple and attack the evil griefers or if they should just escape while they had the chance. He thought about the griefers and how they would attack any innocent person who entered the jungle temple. He asked the group, "Do you think we should go in the temple?"

"Yes!" Henry said gleefully.

"But my village . . ." Georgia was conflicted.

"With Sophie and Tatiana joining us, I'm sure we'll outnumber them and it will be an easy battle," remarked Steve.

Sophie and Tatiana looked at each other, and Sophie said, "I don't think we're equipped to fight anyone. Look at our armor. We're not dressed in diamonds like you guys."

"Well, there's no time to sit around and discuss it," Max said. "We are going to battle these evil rainbow griefers. They've been causing havoc for way too long and they must be stopped."

Max stormed into the jungle temple. A rainbow griefer lunged at him, but Max hit him with his diamond sword. Henry also struck the griefer. It was losing energy quickly.

"I'm going to check the treasure room," Lucy said as the gang fought the griefer. Kyra followed Lucy. They walked around the temple, searching for rainbow griefers in every room and went down the stairs to the bottom floor, where the treasure was stored.

Max, Henry, and Steve followed them down the stairs.

"We destroyed the griefer," Max told them as they made their way toward the treasure.

"What happened to Sophie and Tatiana?" asked Lucy.

"They never came in. I guess they went back home," replied Max.

The bottom floor was empty and the treasure was still there because the puzzle hadn't been solved. The three levers sat on stone bricks and nobody had activated the piston. The group walked past the puzzle and toward the room with the trapped chest, when an army of rainbow griefers ran toward them.

Max skillfully battled the griefers with his diamond sword. Henry threw a potion of slowness on them. Lucy,

Kyra, and Steve fought as many griefers as they could with their swords. Everyone in the gang was struck and losing energy. There were too many griefers and the gang needed help.

They used all of their fighting skills to ward off the griefers, but what they really needed was backup.

Steve knew the battle would be over if they didn't get help. Soon they would all respawn on his wheat farm and they'd have to start all over again. He regretted his decision to fight the evil griefers. He used his remaining energy to destroy a rainbow griefer, when two more rainbow griefers ran down the stairs.

"There are just too many of them!" Max called out. "If only we had more people who could help us, we'd have a chance."

Max's wish was granted. Sophie and Tatiana ran down the stairs and lunged at a group of rainbow griefers. They might have been wearing only leather armor, but they were extremely skilled fighters. With three strikes, they were able to destroy two rainbow griefers.

As Steve battled a rainbow griefer carrying a wooden sword, he was hopeful the gang could win the battle and walk away with the treasure.

6
FLOWER FOREST

The last rainbow griefer was destroyed. The gang stood in front of the treasure.

"We don't want to step on a trip wire and get killed extracting the treasure," Steve warned them. "We need to jump over the trip wire."

Steve took out his pickaxe and broke the stone wall and opened the chest. It contained diamonds and rotten flesh.

"Yuck," Kyra said as she looked at the rotten flesh.

"Who cares about rotten flesh," remarked Lucy. "Look at those blue diamonds."

Steve divided the treasure among the group. "Now you can make diamond armor and swords," Steve said to Tatiana and Sophie.

"Thanks!" said Sophie.

It was almost dusk and the group had to find shelter. "It's almost dark," said Steve. "I think we should stay here."

"Good idea. There are enough torches to protect us from hostile mobs spawning here," said Max.

Sophie and Tatiana walked toward the temple's exit.

"Where are you going?" asked Lucy.

"You've helped us so much," said Tatiana, "but we don't want to intrude any longer."

"We like having you here," said Georgia. "We also like making new friends."

Sophie and Tatiana smiled. "Really?" asked Sophie. "You guys are too nice."

The group waited for dawn. Georgia paced. She was worried about her village. "I wonder what happened tonight and how bad the skeleton attack was on my village."

"What skeleton attack?" asked Sophie.

Georgia told Sophie all about the attacks on her village.

Sophie was upset. "We want to help your village. We had a similar experience. My village was destroyed and only Tatiana and I survived. We used to have a wonderful blacksmith named Eliot and great shops for trading, but now it's burned to the ground. Somebody said Eliot survived, but I'll probably never see him again."

"Eliot!" Steve replied excitedly. "That's the name of the blacksmith in my town."

"Really?" Sophie was surprised. "Maybe he's the same person!"

"Once we help Georgia's village, you should come back to my village and see if he's the same blacksmith.

And you'd love my village. It's very peaceful and everyone is nice. I have a wonderful wheat farm," said Steve.

"That sounds lovely, Steve," said Sophie.

Tatiana added, "It would be nice to have a home again."

"I'm also glad to have the extra help battling these skeletons," Georgia smiled.

The sun began to rise. The group walked out of the jungle temple and was surprised to see the Flower Forest in the distance.

Georgia saw the colorful flowers and shouted, "See, I told you it's not that far away! We're almost there. We can help save the villagers tonight!"

As they approached the Flower Forest, Steve was distracted by the vibrant colors of the red, orange, and pink tulips. Bunnies hopped peacefully in the colorful landscape.

"Bunnies!" Sophie called out. "I wish I had a carrot and then I'd have a new pet."

"Stay away from the rabbits," warned Lucy. "We've encountered a killer rabbit."

"Killer rabbits don't exist," said Tatiana.

"Yes, they do," exclaimed Max. "We were almost killed by a rabbit not too long ago."

Lucy walked around a patch of tulips. "We should pick flowers and use them to make dye. We can dye your leather armor," Lucy told Sophie and Tatiana.

The group picked tulips, sunflowers, and daisies. "We can't spend too much time picking flowers," warned Georgia. "Soon it will be night and we need to get to my village. We still have to make it through the Mesa Biome."

"But the flowers are so beautiful. I wish we could stay longer," said Kyra.

Max thought he saw something move behind the colorful flowers, but he assumed it was a bunny.

Steve walked closer to the patch of flowers where Max had seen the moving creature. Steve began to pick the flowers, and Max called out, "Steve, be careful!"

It was too late. A rainbow griefer approached Steve and struck him with his diamond sword. Steve's health bar was low and the single blow destroyed him.

"Steve!" Lucy shouted.

"Where is he?" asked Kyra.

Max charged at the rainbow griefer and struck him with his diamond sword. The rest of the gang leaped at the griefer. The rainbow griefer was surrounded and destroyed.

"I can't believe Steve is gone," Lucy began to cry.

"He probably respawned at Kyra's house. He'll never be able to make it back here in time," said Georgia.

Max walked over to the patch of flowers to pick up Steve's stuff. He returned to the group, holding Steve's sword.

"It's Steve's diamond sword," Lucy cried. "He worked so hard to make that sword and get the diamonds. All he wanted to do was save his village from the zombie attack and now he doesn't have the sword. Even if he tries to make his way here, he will have no way to protect himself."

"What can we do?" asked Henry.

"Should we go back to the wheat farm?" asked Kyra.

"I'm conflicted," remarked Georgia. "I want to help Steve and I need to save my village. This is so upsetting."

Max held up Steve's diamond armor. "Steve also needs this, too. Poor guy. He must be heartbroken over what happened."

"I know," Lucy sympathized.

An arrow shot at the group. "Oh no!" Max called out. "More rainbow griefers!"

Kyra contemplated getting destroyed by the rainbow griefer, so she could help Steve at the wheat farm, but Max destroyed the rainbow griefer with two blows. He was a skilled swordsman.

The group looked out for other rainbow griefers in the distance, and it looked like they were all gone.

Max saw something move and took out his bow and arrow and began to shoot.

"Stop! No arrows," a familiar voice called out.

"Steve!" Kyra exclaimed.

"How did you get here?" Georgia was shocked.

"My friend Alex taught me how to TP. That was the first time I have ever teleported; I felt like an Enderman. I'm so glad it worked. Now I can help you guys battle these evil skeletons," Steve said with a smile.

Henry ran over to Steve, but an arrow flew between them. The battle of the rainbow griefers had just started.

7
MADDENING MOBS

The rainbow griefers shot many volleys of arrows. Lucy was hit, but only weakened. The others avoided the sea of arrows that flew in their direction. Steve took out a potion of harming from his inventory and threw it at the griefers. The griefers didn't have enough energy to shoot at Steve and his friends.

"It's time to escape!" Steve told his friends.

"I'm not letting these griefers get away." Henry sped toward the rainbow griefers and struck one with his diamond sword.

Steve and the others followed Henry, using whatever weapons they had available. Within minutes the griefers were destroyed.

"Let's head toward the Mesa Biome," instructed Henry.

The group trekked through the flower-laden land to a landscape with sparse shrubbery and flowers. The reddish clay blocks varied in shades of brown and red. Steve climbed up a hill with his friends.

"It's right over there!" Georgia could see her village from the top of the hill. "It looks like some of the shops burned down. Somebody must have used TNT."

"Soon you'll be reunited with your friends and you can save your village," said Lucy.

Steve took out his pickaxe and banged into the clay ground.

"What are you doing?" asked Kyra.

"This clay is fantastic to build with. Georgia, you should take some too." Steve knew Georgia was also an expert builder. He met Georgia as a fellow participant at a building contest on Mushroom Island.

Steve placed the clay in his inventory, when he noticed red sand. "We can use this sand, too."

The group joined Steve and began to collect clay and sand. "I want to give you all my clay, so you can build something really cool in our village," Kyra said as she gathered clay blocks.

They were almost finished mining the clay when Georgia said, "I think we will make it to my village before nightfall. I'm thrilled."

"We should get going," Steve told them.

They climbed up a hill. "It's right over this rise," Georgia informed them.

As they reached the bottom of the hill, there was a flash of blue light across the sky.

"What was that?" wondered Lucy.

She didn't need to hear a response. Instantly a three-headed wither spawned in front of the group. The wither made a loud sound as it flew through the skies of the Mesa Biome.

"The rainbow griefer probably sent it here!" screamed Sophie. "What should we do?"

"What did we do last time?" Georgia asked, trying to remember her one and only encounter with the wither. This happened when they were at the building competition and another griefer had summoned it to destroy the contest.

"Get your bows and arrows out now!" shouted Lucy. "We need to attack the wither before it destroys us!"

"Don't shoot yet!" Max informed them. "When it first spawns, arrows can't damage it. The wither is still spawning. It has to grow stronger."

Once the wither shot its first exploding wither skull out of one of its three heads, Max shouted, "Go! Now!"

"Sophie and Tatiana," Henry yelled, "hide behind the hill when you fight. Your leather armor isn't strong enough to withstand a blow from a wither skull."

Max shot arrows as fast as he could, but even with perfect aim it was hard to hit the wither. The wither flew through the sky and shot wither skulls at the group. An exploding skull hit Kyra.

"Kyra, are you okay?" Lucy called out as she shot as many arrows as she could at the fierce floating menace.

"I think so," replied Kyra.

"You need to get milk from your inventory," Max called to Kyra. "It helps you recover from a wither attack."

Kyra drank the milk and gathered up enough energy to shoot an arrow at the flying black creature.

Although the wither's energy was diminishing from the arrows, it still had a lot of strength. The wither made piercing sounds as the skulls exploded. It seemed as if this was an impossible battle, and the group worried they'd lose the fight. They were so close to Georgia's village and now it could all be over. Within seconds they could all be back on the wheat farm.

The blue and black wither skulls continued to explode nearby the group. The gang continued to defend themselves by shooting arrows at the flying creature. They used all of their arrows as the wither's health began to deteriorate.

Lucy ran toward the floating three-headed wither and threw a potion of healing on it, and the wither's health rapidly diminished. Max shot another arrow. Again, the wither shot another exploding skull, but Sophie threw a bucket of water at it. The wither tried to fight back, but it was too weak.

"You can't shoot arrows at it anymore. We have to use swords," Max told them, as he charged at the wither and struck it with his diamond sword. "Make sure you have milk handy. It will heal you from the wither effect," he continued.

Each person in the group took turns striking the wither and retreating, until the wither was destroyed.

The wither made a large noise that boomed through the biome and disappeared. A Nether star dropped on the ground.

"Finally!" Georgia was excited. "We should head to my village right now—we don't have much time before nightfall."

But they were too late. Nightfall had set in, and the group picked up their pace as they moved toward the town. They needed to seek shelter in Georgia's house and sleep.

Boom! They heard an explosion in the distance.

"What was that?" asked Lucy.

"I don't know," said Georgia nervously, "but it sounded like it was coming from my village."

8

SKELETON SOLDIERS

As night set in, Georgia hurried to her house. "It's right over there!" she called to the others. The group walked up to a mansion; it was enormous and made of quartz.

"Wow, this is so fancy!" exclaimed Lucy. She had never seen a house that nice before and was excited to stay there.

Max lit a torch and placed it on the quartz wall.

"Look at your farm!" Steve walked over to Georgia's farm. An explosion had destroyed most of the farm, leaving just charred grass and a few crops that were wilting.

"That's probably the work of a griefer," remarked Henry. "A griefer with TNT."

"It looks more like the result of a creeper explosion to me," said Kyra.

"In any case, we'll need to help you rebuild your farm," said Steve.

"I don't see any skeletons," remarked Lucy. "Maybe we missed the attack."

"Let's get to bed," Georgia said and invited them into her house. The living room had a large fountain and picture window that looked out at the burnt farm. The scenic tan-colored hills from the Mesa Biome could be seen in the distance. The group toured the house, walking on the diamond ore floor and stopping to look at the many fireplaces in each room.

Georgia led them up the stairs. "You can each have your own room."

"Our own room?" Max questioned. "We usually just get our own bed."

"Well, here you can have your own room if you'd like," Georgia told them as they each chose a bedroom and curled up in bed.

When they awoke, Georgia asked her friends to join her in the kitchen. Chests filled with food sat atop the kitchen's granite countertops. She offered the gang some cake. As they chowed down on the yummy eats, the group came up with a plan.

"What time do the skeletons usually arrive?" asked Henry, looking out the window.

"Right before the sun sets," replied Georgia.

Max could see villagers rushing past Georgia's window. "Well, I think the skeletons are here now. We need to help!"

"That's weird. It's daytime," remarked Steve.

Max ran to the door as raindrops pelted his helmet. "It's raining! The skeletons can live in the rain because of the lack of sunlight."

The group suited up and sprinted toward the village as rain pounded down on them.

Georgia didn't exaggerate; there were dozens of skeletons shooting arrows at the residents.

One of Georgia's neighbors used TNT to fight the bony creatures and destroyed a cluster of skeletons.

"I wonder if that person is responsible for destroying your farm," Steve said, pointing out the neighbor with the TNT.

"That's my neighbor, Nia. She has been fighting the skeletons with me. If she did blow up my farm, it was probably an accident that happened while trying to kill skeletons."

Georgia raced to Nia. Nia was excited to see that Georgia had returned. "You can help us battle the skeletons," said Nia.

"I brought friends," Georgia told Nia.

"Great, we need all the help we can get—the skeleton invasion is getting worse. And now we have a day invasion, after weeks of nightly attacks. This is unbelievable. I'm going to run out of TNT."

An army of skeletons descended upon the group. Max shot arrows and Kyra threw a potion of harming at the walking dead mob. As they destroyed skeletons, the creatures dropped bones and arrows on the ground.

"The TNT destroys more of them. You'll get nowhere if you just use a bow and arrow," Nia said, while blowing up the skeletons with a block of TNT.

Hordes of skeletons surged down the hill as Nia attacked and destroyed them with TNT.

"Good job," exclaimed Max.

"It looks like you figured out a plan for survival," said Georgia.

"I don't consider blowing up an army of skeletons as surviving; it's barely existing. I spend all day preparing for this evening invasion. I can't farm. I can't build." Nia was upset and exhausted.

"It looks like the sun is coming out. Let's go back to my place and figure out a plan," suggested Georgia.

The rain cleared and the group walked back to Georgia's palatial home. They started talking as they walked through the door. They had to solve this problem, and every one of them had a theory on who or what was causing these skeleton invasions.

"There has to be somebody behind this invasion. Skeletons don't usually just attack in such large quantities each night," theorized Max.

"But who would do this? We have such a peaceful village." Georgia couldn't believe somebody would target her town.

"Maybe the culprit is jealous because you live in such a nice village," said Sophie.

"That could be, but we need to figure out who is behind this and how we can stop it." Georgia was serious. She was fed up with the attacks.

"Oh no!" Max called out. "Look outside the window! It's raining again and there are more skeletons."

"It's never-ending." Nia was exhausted but took up her TNT and made to go outside and face the skeletons.

The others followed Nia. They carried bows and arrows and swords. The skeletons spotted the group emerging from Georgia's house and unleashed a flurry of arrows.

"Look at that green—" said Lucy, but Georgia interrupted her.

"A creeper!" Georgia burst out.

"Stand back!" Max exclaimed as he brushed water from his cheek.

"If the rain doesn't stop, we'll be fighting forever," Nia said, grabbing a block of TNT.

Lightning struck the creeper, charging it and making it extremely potent. The creeper silently headed toward Georgia's house. On the path to Georgia's farm, the creeper had a run-in with a skeleton.

Kaboom! The creeper exploded and destroyed three skeletons.

"At least your farm was already burned to the ground," remarked Steve. The rain was getting heavier and thunder boomed throughout the village.

"Should we go to your house?" asked Lucy.

"No, we have to fight these skeletons," Georgia replied.

Nia used the TNT to destroy another group of skeletons.

"I don't see any more skeletons," said Max as he looked into the distance.

"Maybe this invasion is finally over for the night," Georgia said.

"Wishful thinking," replied Steve as he pointed out another group of skeletons walking toward them. One of them shot an arrow at Steve, and it landed on his chest.

"I'm running low on energy," Steve worried aloud.

Max struck one of the skeletons and destroyed it. The gang shot arrows at the skeletons until they defeated the mob.

"Finally, we can head home," said Kyra. "The rain is letting up, and the sun is coming out. Now we can make another plan."

"Yes, we need a plan. My TNT attack strategy isn't working," said Nia.

"We don't have much time. We lost a portion of the morning due to the rain," Georgia told them as she opened the door to her home.

This time when they entered the home, they weren't as chatty. They were exhausted. They needed to come up with a strategy, but they were at a loss for ideas.

The group stood by Georgia's fireplace, enjoying the warmth after the rain, when they heard voices outside the door.

"Who's there?" Georgia called out.

9
UNLIKELY ALLIES

"Maybe it's just my neighbors," Georgia said as she walked to the door. "We've been having meetings about the skeleton attack."

"You should look out the window," warned Nia, "the meetings aren't happening anymore. People are getting vicious and nobody can be trusted."

Georgia peeked out the window, trying to catch a glimpse of who stood outside her door.

"I don't know who they are," Georgia said in a worried tone. "Should I open it?"

"Yes, but we have to be prepared," instructed Lucy.

The group got their weapons ready. Georgia put on her armor and opened the door.

"Stop! Don't attack!" a person in a blue-dyed leather helmet called out.

"We need help." His friend, wearing dyed-orange leather armor, called to them.

"Why?" Georgia pointed her diamond sword at the strangers.

The person wearing the blue helmet confessed to the group, "Our friends turned against us because we didn't like what they were doing, and we began to question them."

Steve walked toward the door. "What were your friends doing that you didn't like?"

"They have—" the blue-helmeted person began, but his companion in the orange armor interrupted.

"We just need your help. We can't tell you why," he said.

"Do you have names?" asked Lucy.

"I'm Dylan," said the person in orange.

"I'm Liam," his friend wearing the blue helmet told the group.

"We know who is behind the skeleton attack," Dylan stated as he walked into Georgia's house.

"And we know how to stop it," added Liam.

"Why do you need our help?" asked Georgia.

"We need your help because we are afraid we will be attacked. We need backup. If you follow us to the jungle, we'll show you where the skeletons are coming from," said Dylan.

"We used to be griefers," confessed Liam.

"How do we know you're not griefers planning to trick us?" Steve questioned their motives.

"You don't." Dylan looked at the group. "You'll just have to trust us."

"Who is going to attack you?" asked Lucy.

"The rainbow griefers. They are the ones controlling the skeletons. We can't fight them alone," said Liam.

"How do you know this?" Georgia was suspicious. She had never seen these two people in her town before, and she wondered why they had so much information about the skeleton attack.

"We can't tell you. You just have to help us." Dylan walked out the door. "Follow us and we'll lead you to the griefers."

Steve and the others knew the rainbow griefers could be the evil culprits behind the attack, but they were also suspicious of Liam and Dylan. However, since they had no other plan, they decided to follow Dylan and Liam to the rainbow griefers.

"We also need to eat. We've been battling skeletons all morning and we are all low on energy," Steve told them.

"There isn't much time," warned Dylan. "It's almost nightfall. I know how we can stop tonight's skeleton attack."

The group quickly ate fruit from the chest in Georgia's kitchen. "We can't fight with a depleted food bar," Georgia told them, taking a bite of an apple.

Dylan and Liam were impatient. They paced as the group ate, and then ran out of the house, shouting, "Follow us!"

"To the jungle!" instructed Liam.

The gang sprinted through the village, past the shops and the villagers, the Mesa Biome, and the Flower Forest, toward the lush jungle.

"Stick close together," Max shouted to his friends. "It's hard to see through these leaves."

Georgia worried that Liam and Dylan were leading them into a trap. This was the same jungle where they had battled the rainbow griefers at the temple.

"This looks familiar," Steve said as they approached the jungle temple.

"Watch out!" screamed Sophie.

A horde of rainbow griefers burst out of the temple, shooting arrows at the group. Max and Tatiana were struck. Two griefers struck a weakened Max and Tatiana with their diamond swords, destroying them.

"Oh no!" Georgia called out in horror, as two rainbow griefers raced toward her with their diamond swords. She was no match for these powerful griefers.

Rainbow griefers cornered Lucy and Kyra. There was no escape.

The sun was setting as Sophie battled the griefers. She was so preoccupied with her battle that she neglected to notice a creeper sidle up to her.

Kaboom! The creeper exploded. The fiery beast destroyed Sophie and the evil griefers.

Only Henry and Steve remained. They tried to battle the griefers, but they were outnumbered. And they were also worried about their friends. This battle was horrendous. They needed help.

Henry struck a rainbow griefer with his diamond sword, but five rainbow griefers shot arrows at him and he couldn't fight back. Henry was gone and only Steve and his new friends, Liam and Dylan, were left to battle these evil rainbow men.

Steve struck a griefer, as Liam and Dylan hurried toward Steve's side.

"Great, you guys are going to help me!" Steve said as a group of griefers charged at him.

"Yeah, we'll help you," Dylan laughed as he struck Steve with his diamond sword, and Steve was destroyed.

10
START OVER

Steve awoke in a strange bedroom. *Where am I?* he asked himself as he walked around the room. He could hear familiar voices outside the door. He walked toward the door and listened. It was Max and Henry. Steve could hear them talking about Dylan and Liam, questioning if they were okay and whether they had survived the attack.

Steve realized the strange bedroom was in Georgia's house. This was the last place he slept. He opened the door and saw Max and Henry.

"Steve!" Henry exclaimed. "So good to see you!"

"Everyone was destroyed in that rainbow griefer attack," said Max.

"Where is everybody else?" asked Steve.

"They're in the kitchen," replied Henry.

Steve found his friends in Georgia's kitchen and asked, "Is it morning?"

"Yes," Georgia laughed, "but that's not important. We need to know how everyone is feeling. Yesterday was intense."

"I lost my diamond sword," Steve cried out. "When I was destroyed, they took it from me! Now the rainbow griefers have my sword."

"We all lost our weapons," said Henry. "It's awful."

"Don't worry, I have diamonds and we can craft new swords," Georgia told them.

"Enough for all of us?" asked Sophie.

"Yeah, we have the diamonds from the temple!" remembered Steve.

"I put them in a chest by my enchanting table," Georgia told them, and the gang followed Georgia to the area where she kept her enchanting table and anvil. She opened the chest.

"It's empty!" Lucy cried out. "Somebody must have stolen the diamonds when we were fighting."

"I wonder what else they took," said Georgia as she walked to the chest she kept in her bedroom, which was filled with armor and potions. She opened it, and it was also emptied. She gasped. "I have nothing!"

"I think we might have to go mining," Henry told them.

Steve wanted his diamond sword. Even if he found a million diamonds, he could never make a sword that was as meaningful as the diamond sword he had worked so hard to create. Also, Steve knew finding diamonds wasn't easy. "How are we going to find enough diamonds to make swords?" he wondered.

"I know a great mine outside the village. If we mine there, we might find a bunch of diamonds. It's our only hope," replied Georgia.

The group suited up for mining and held pickaxes as they silently trekked toward the mine. Everyone's spirits were down.

Finally Lucy spoke, breaking the silence. "What happened to Dylan and Liam?"

"They destroyed me," Steve informed the group. "They weren't our friends. They tricked us. They work with the rainbow griefers."

"I knew it!" Georgia exclaimed.

"I suspected it, too," added Steve, "but I didn't think they'd destroy me with their diamond swords."

"I bet they have all of our stuff," theorized Georgia. "If we find them, we won't have to mine for diamonds."

The mine was just a few feet away.

"We need to mine for diamonds. We need to have powerful swords to battle Dylan and Liam," Henry said as he walked into the mine.

"Look out!" Max called out.

"Rainbow griefers?" asked Henry.

"No, a cave spider!" Kyra grabbed a wooden sword from her inventory and smashed the spider.

"I'm sure there are more. We have to be on the lookout, since this mine is in a cave," Sophie said as she hit the ground with her pickaxe, hoping they would find diamonds quickly and could leave the creepy mine.

The group dug deep within the ground. The first layer revealed stone.

"Coal," Max pointed out. "We should put this in our inventory. Let's mine it."

The group dug deeper into the stone, finding iron and redstone, but no diamonds.

"Blue!" Lucy shouted. "I see blue."

The group gathered their remaining strength and dug until they reached a bunch of diamonds.

"We need to put these in our inventory and craft new swords at your house," Henry told Georgia.

The group rushed out of the mine, when Liam and Dylan stopped them. They stood at the entrance of the mine, pointing diamond swords at the group.

"Give us your diamonds," demanded Liam.

"Never!" screamed Georgia.

"I want my diamond sword back!" Steve was furious. "You stole all of our stuff and you tricked us," he angrily accused them. "I'd rather die than give you anything else."

"We can grant that wish," Dylan said as he advanced toward Steve.

Sophie blocked Steve. She took out an iron ax and struck Dylan.

"Thanks!" said Steve.

Nia took her bow and arrow and shot at Dylan, while Max and Henry battled Liam with their wooden swords. This time the two tricksters didn't have their rainbow griefers as backup and sprinted away.

The group walked back toward Georgia's village, when they were stopped in their tracks by an enormous bedrock wall.

"What's this?" asked Lucy. "I don't remember seeing this on our way here. "

"I think we are trapped," said Steve as he walked along the wall and realized they were trapped in a box of bedrock.

"How are we going to get out of here?" asked Georgia.

"I have TNT," replied Nia.

"That doesn't work. Only the cube of destruction works, but we'd all get destroyed. And I don't even have the materials to make it," explained Steve.

"There's no ceiling," remarked Henry. "Are you thinking what I'm thinking?"

"Yeah!" replied Max.

Henry and Max said in unison, "We can build our way out of here!"

They used cobblestone blocks that reached the top of the wall. Then they each jumped down, landing safely on the other side of the wall. They rushed back to Georgia's house as dusk was beginning to set.

"I see skeletons!" Lucy shouted.

"We're going to have to battle them without diamond swords. It's going to be a challenge, but we can do it," said Steve.

The group gathered weapons from their inventory, as the skeletons shot a flurry of arrows at them.

Tatiana was hit by two arrows and was very weak. The skeletons advanced toward her. Lucy jumped in front of the pack of skeletons and lunged at them with her iron sword, striking the bony creatures.

"Take this!" Nia shouted as she placed TNT near a group of skeletons and activated it with flint and steel.

Steve hurtled toward a skeleton. He struck it with his wooden sword. He looked into the skeleton's sad eyes and wondered why the skeleton was attacking them. Maybe this wasn't the skeleton's fault. Maybe they were fighting someone else's battle? Steve knew he had to find out where the skeletons were coming from. Once he did, there was hope this battle could finally end.

The gang was defeating the skeletons and they were ready to head back to Georgia's house to sleep. Once the final skeleton was destroyed, they all felt relieved until Henry called out.

"It's a zombie invasion!"

The exhausted group watched as five zombies wobbled toward them.

"It's going to be a long night," Max exclaimed.

11
HIDDEN FARM

The green block-headed zombies emerged from a hill behind Georgia's house. These vacant-eyed creatures didn't notice Steve and his friends and walked past them as they headed toward the village.

"That's a relief," said Sophie.

"A relief? We have to help the villagers!" protested Georgia.

"We lost our iron golem during one of the skeleton attacks," added Nia. "They'll have no protection."

The villagers' cries were heard in the distance. The group ran to help.

"How are we going to do this? We have no energy and limited resources for fighting." Henry was worried they were trekking toward a losing battle. He was tired of being defeated.

"We have to try. They need our help!" Steve exclaimed as he ran.

As they approached the village, the gang struck zombies with wooden swords, iron swords, a pickaxe, and TNT.

A purple-clad zombie ripped a door off the library and attacked the librarian, turning her into a zombie villager.

Max gave the librarian a golden apple to reverse the effects of the zombie attack. He watched as she ate it and recovered.

"We can do this," Georgia said as she clobbered a zombie with her sword.

More zombies roamed through the ravaged village streets. Lucy tried to fight off three zombies with a wooden sword, but needed backup. Kyra joined Lucy in her battle. Meanwhile, Max struck two zombies with his sword.

"I can't do this anymore!" Tatiana cried out.

"It's almost over," Sophie reassured her.

The sun began to rise and the creatures of the night were destroyed. Exhausted, the group walked back to Georgia's house. In the distance, they could see a person running toward them. She was wearing a pink helmet and carried a diamond sword. Max aimed his bow and arrow at her, but Georgia screamed, "No! She's my neighbor, Olive. Max, stop! Please don't shoot!"

"I have important news," Olive called out.

Georgia invited her into the house. As they munched on baked potatoes, Olive told them about a hidden farm.

"I was walking to the village, when I saw a group of rainbow griefers. I took shelter behind a tree, and they didn't see me, but I could hear them. They were talking about a secret farm where they are spawning skeletons. We have to find it."

"Do you know where this secret farm is located in the jungle?" asked Georgia.

"No. I snuck away when I realized the rainbow griefers didn't know I was there," Olive told them.

Steve asked, "Do the skeletons come from the same direction each night?"

"Yes, from over the hill," replied Nia.

"That's the same direction as the jungle. I bet they have the farm there. That's where we saw the rainbow griefers by the jungle temple," said Georgia. She was excited they might be able to find the hidden farm.

"Let's head to the jungle. Who knows, the spawner could be in the jungle temple," said Henry.

"We can't go unless we craft diamond swords and armor," Lucy reminded them.

The group took out their diamonds, walked to Georgia's crafting table, and constructed their new diamond swords and armor. They used Georgia's enchanting table to enchant the swords.

"How do I look?" asked Georgia when they were all done.

"You look like you're ready to stop the griefers and their skeleton army," Henry told her and hurried out the door toward the jungle.

The group kept watch for rainbow griefers. Unlike the way they had hidden themselves in the colorful flower forest, the rainbow griefers couldn't camouflage themselves in the green leaves. They were easy to spot. The gang walked slowly; they didn't want to miss the entrance to the farm. The leaves were thick and they couldn't see very well.

"Don't we have to turn left?" asked Max. "I remember the temple was by this patch of trees."

"Everything looks alike," remarked Henry. "I'm not sure where we are going."

The group heard a noise.

"Shh!" Lucy whispered. "I think I hear something."

The gang listened and heard Liam and Dylan talking.

"I love my new sword," said Dylan.

As the gang hid behind a thick patch of leaves, they could see Liam and Dylan play-fighting with their stolen diamond swords.

"I want my sword back," Steve muttered to the group.

"Shh!" Lucy warned him. "Be quiet or they'll hear us. If we follow them, maybe they'll lead us to the skeleton farm. That's more important than battling them for our swords."

Steve knew Lucy was right, but he still really wanted his sword back. His sword was once stolen by his old neighbor Thomas, the griefer. Steve fought to get his sword back when Thomas stole it, and he wasn't going to give it up now. Steve promised himself that once they found the skeleton farm, he'd fight for it. He needed his sword.

Liam and Dylan continued to play-fight, as the group looked on from the safety of the leaves.

"Look, they're heading toward the water," Tatiana pointed out.

The group followed them.

"Oh no!" Kyra cried out.

A group of rainbow griefers raced toward Liam and Dylan, waving diamond swords at them.

"Traitors!" one of the rainbow griefers shouted at Liam and Dylan.

"We didn't do anything," Dylan protested.

"That's not what people are saying," another rainbow griefer screamed, and struck Liam with his sword.

"What are you talking about?" questioned Liam.

"We would never betray you," cried Dylan.

"You gave away important secrets." A rainbow griefer struck Dylan with his sword.

Liam and Dylan tried to sprint away and headed in the direction of the group.

"What should we do?" Kyra said in a panic.

"Nothing. Let's just stay still and hope they don't see us," Henry informed them.

The group stood still and held their breaths as Liam and Dylan raced past them. The rainbow griefers didn't even bother to chase them.

"I wonder what that was all about," questioned Sophie.

"I don't know, but they did something to make the rainbow griefers angry. And I wonder if it had anything to do with us," said Steve.

"We need to keep going. We have to find that temple," Henry said as he walked farther into the jungle.

A wild ocelot bounded past them.

"Ignore it," Steve instructed them. "This is no time for distractions. We have to get to the temple."

Leaves surrounded them as they walked along the river toward the jungle temple.

"I think it's right over there! On the water!" Lucy was excited.

They hurried toward the temple. They were just a few steps away from the entrance when a barrage of arrows stopped them.

12
LOST IN THE JUNGLE

An arrow struck Sophie's diamond armor and slid off. "Wow, this works so much better than my old leather armor!"

Despite being dressed in armor, the group ran from the arrows. Max stayed back and shot an arrow that landed on the ground. He wasn't certain what he was aiming for and admitted, "I don't see anybody."

"Who shot the arrows?" asked Tatiana.

"I'm not sure. I don't see any rainbow griefers," remarked Henry.

The group sheared the leaves, clearing a path to see what enemy attacked them, but there was nobody there.

"Should we head back to the temple?" asked Kyra.

"We sprinted so fast and so far away—which way is the temple?" Georgia questioned. She hadn't been keeping track of where she was going; she just had wanted to escape the sea of arrows.

"I'm not sure." Max looked out at the path and didn't see the river or the temple.

"Oh no!" cried Kyra. "We're lost."

"Don't worry. We'll find our way," Max assured her as he explored the area. "I think we just have to head this way." He walked down a path filled with leaves.

"It's getting dark," Olive announced.

"I think it's just the leaves; if we cut them down, we'll have more light." Steve cut the leaves down to reveal a setting sun.

"Great. Now we're trapped in the jungle and we're a target for hostile mobs roaming around." Georgia was exhausted.

It was dark. The group huddled together searching for hostile mobs that were ready to attack them.

Kaboom! The group heard an explosion.

"That doesn't sound like a creeper. It sounds like something more sinister, like TNT," remarked Henry.

"It's probably the rainbow griefers. Maybe they're clearing land to build something," said Max.

"I'm scared." Sophie's voice quavered.

"We're all scared, but if we stick together, we'll be fine," Max reassured her.

Click. Clang.

"Do you hear that?" Tatiana was petrified and could barely speak.

The loud sound of rattling bones made the leaves shake and left the group terrified.

Sophie peeked out from behind the tree and whispered, "It looks like there are hundreds of skeletons marching in a row."

"I've never seen that many skeletons in my life. I wonder where they're going," said Tatiana.

"I'm sure they are headed toward the village. We have to get back there and help!" Georgia wanted to rush back and save her friends.

"No, we have to find out where they're coming from, so we can stop them from spawning," Steve reminded them.

The row of skeletons seemed never-ending. The bony white mob marched in an orderly line. The group watched in both terror and awe.

"If they are headed to the village, this is going to be the worst invasion the villagers have ever seen." Nia knew battling hundreds of skeletons was impossible. "The village will be destroyed tonight."

"Should we try fighting some of them?" asked Kyra.

"No, follow me," Henry directed as he walked quietly, hiding behind the trees. "We need to find out where they are spawning."

Two pairs of purple eyes glowed in the night sky.

"It's Endermen," Steve called to the group. "Don't stare or provoke them."

It was too late. One of the Endermen had locked eyes with Sophie and was shrieking as it teleported toward her.

The skeletons heard the noise from the Enderman and rushed toward the group. Sophie ran, hoping to find the river. The group followed her, as they shot arrows at the skeletons.

The Enderman's shrieks grew louder, and Sophie ran as fast as she could toward the river.

"The river is right over there, beyond those trees," shouted Max as he took aim at a skeleton.

Sophie grabbed a potion of water breathing from her inventory and plunged into the deep blue water. The Enderman followed her into the water and was destroyed.

The others had no way of fighting this powerful army of skeletons. They followed Sophie and drank potions of water breathing and jumped into the river.

"Sophie," Lucy called out, "where are you?"

The group swam deep into the river looking for Sophie. They found her swimming by a squid.

"We have to stay down here as long as possible," said Henry. "We don't want to be victims of the skeletons."

Georgia wondered if they should just battle the skeletons. If they were destroyed, they'd just wind up in her house. Then she remembered they would lose their diamond swords, and they didn't have any diamonds left.

The water was calm and it was very quiet. "It's peaceful," Tatiana said as she swam around the group.

Arrows flew through the water and one struck Henry.

"They're shooting at us!" screamed Lucy.

"We have to fight back!" Steve swam to the surface and took out his diamond sword. He was ready to battle the bony creatures. The group followed, as they swam to the shore and began the battle of their lives.

13
DUNGEONS

The skeletons shot arrows, but were distracted as a wolf rushed past them.

Click! Clack! Clang! The bony beings fled from the wolf.

"That's right," remarked Steve. "They're afraid of wolves."

The sun began to rise. "We're safe!" Lucy was excited the battle was over before it really even began.

"Now we can find that temple," said Max. "Which way should we go?"

Georgia replied, "I'm pretty sure we just head down this path." They followed Georgia as she walked down a tree-lined path.

"I see it!" shouted Max. The majestic temple stood in front of the group.

"Look!" Sophie called out.

Liam and Dylan were standing in front of the temple. They had their diamond swords out.

"It looks like they're guarding it," remarked Steve.

"I wonder if they are guarding it from us or from the rainbow griefers," added Georgia.

"If they are guarding it, I bet there is something important in there," Sophie suggested as she walked toward the temple.

"Watch out," warned Tatiana. "You don't want them to see you."

Without warning Steve impetuously flew toward Liam and Dylan shouting, "I want my diamond sword back, you thieves!"

"Look who it is, Liam," Dylan stated as he pointed the diamond sword at Steve. "Yes, this is your sword, and it's fantastic."

"Do you want to fight us? Because we can destroy you and take your new sword," said Steve. Liam just laughed.

"You're bullies. I'm not afraid of you!" Steve lunged at Dylan and struck him with his sword.

Liam hit Steve. "This is a losing battle," Liam said as he struck Steve again.

Max shot an arrow at Liam.

"He has his friends with him!" Dylan noted when he saw the group sprinting toward them.

Lucy hit Liam with her diamond sword. "What's so valuable that you're guarding this temple? Tell me!"

"Stop! Don't hurt us. This wasn't even our idea. It's all the rainbow griefers' idea. We are their prisoners," confessed Dylan.

"How can we believe you?" questioned Steve.

"They are keeping us prisoner here. They want us to lead their skeleton army. We just want to go back to our village." Liam begged the gang to stop hitting him with the sword and pleaded, "I have very little energy left."

"If we are destroyed, we'll respawn in the prison the rainbow griefers put us in. It's in a dirty dungeon with cave spiders," Dylan told the group.

"Why were you so mean to me? Why did you steal my sword?" Steve's sword was inches from Dylan's face. One more strike and Dylan would be destroyed and would possibly respawn in the prison.

"Take it back," offered Dylan. He handed the sword to Steve. "Put it in your inventory quickly before the rainbow griefers see us. Just let us leave. Please."

Steve grabbed the sword and placed it in his inventory. He was pleased to have the sword back, but he was still upset by Liam and Dylan's behavior. He was also very confused. He wondered if Liam and Dylan were tricking the group again. He still wasn't quite clear about their motives.

"Please, let us escape," Liam pleaded. "We need to get out of here before the rainbow griefers return."

"No," demanded Henry, "come with us." Henry held a sword close to Dylan as he forced them to enter the jungle temple.

"We know there is a skeleton spawner down here," warned Steve.

The group walked into the main room of the enormous temple. "We need to go downstairs. That's where a spawner is usually set up," Max said as they held their swords at Liam's and Dylan's backs.

"You don't want to go downstairs," warned Dylan. "The rainbow griefers will attack us and anyway there's nothing down there; the griefers emptied the treasure."

"Let's all escape together and get away from these griefers," added Liam.

"I can't abandon my village!" Georgia said defiantly.

"Neither can we!" Nia and Olive said in unison.

"Well, there are no skeletons down here," said Dylan. "There's nothing down here."

Dylan and Liam were correct—the treasure had been looted, but Steve and his friends were the ones who took it, after they battled the rainbow griefers. Steve was pretty sure these two tricksters, Dylan and Liam, were the culprits behind the heist at Georgia's house, and were probably in possession of the treasure.

Steve walked past a lever, stopping to inspect it. "What's this?" he questioned.

"It's nothing," remarked Dylan.

"If it's nothing then why don't you pull it?" demanded Steve.

"No!" Liam screamed as Dylan pulled the lever, and a piston door opened. The group was shocked. The room was packed with skeletons.

Two creepers silently made their way into the skeleton-filled room.

Kaboom! The skeletons killed the creepers. Two CDs dropped to the floor.

"Don't pick them up. You don't want the skeletons to see you," Georgia called out to her friends.

Dylan and Liam reached for the discs, and Steve charged toward them. The skeletons grew hostile and shot arrows at the group.

Max placed a torch on the wall. "Guys, get your torches out! We can make it so light in here that we stop the skeletons!"

The gang placed torches and the skeletons retreated.

"This is such a crazy place," Tatiana exclaimed as she explored the skeleton farm. A cage sat in the center of the room and it led to a machine, which destroyed the skeletons.

"This must be where the bones drop," Steve said when he walked into the kill room.

"Watch out!" Lucy screamed, as a pack of rainbow griefers rushed toward Steve. "They might throw you in the lava!"

Steve looked behind him to see a man-made lava river running through the skeleton farm.

Max hurried toward the rainbow griefers and with all his might struck as many as he could, but he was outnumbered. Two rainbow griefers teamed up and hit Max with their swords. It was too much for him. Max's diamond sword dropped to the ground.

"Max!" Henry screamed, and raced to grab the sword, but a rainbow griefer had already picked it up.

Henry struck the rainbow griefer and destroyed it. "I have Max's sword! I will bring it back to him!" Henry was thrilled, and he struck another rainbow griefer.

Liam rushed at Henry, clobbering him with his diamond sword.

"I knew it!" Henry said weakly. "I knew you were on their side."

14

BAD TO THE BONE

Arrows shot through the skeleton farm and swords clanged. Yet the gang was not fighting skeletons. They were in an intense battle with rainbow griefers. Liam and Dylan joined the rainbow griefers in a fight against Steve and his friends. No matter how many griefers were destroyed, there was always a new crop surging down the stairs, ready to attack.

Tatiana's health bar was extremely low. One more hit from a griefer and she would be destroyed. She tried to grab a piece of fruit from her inventory, but a rainbow griefer struck her and she dropped the fruit and her sword.

Steve used his remaining energy to destroy a griefer. Henry took out a potion of weakness and splashed it on the griefers. "Now is our chance!"

The group charged at the griefers, striking as many as they could.

Liam and Dylan were in the corner of the room and avoided being splashed with the potion. They both drank a potion of swiftness and sprinted toward Steve.

"Game over!" they shouted as they tag teamed Steve and he was destroyed.

Steve awoke in his bed at Georgia's house. Max and Tatiana were in the kitchen, refueling.

"They got my sword," Max told Steve.

"Mine too." Tatiana was upset.

"Don't worry. I know Henry was able to save your sword, Max. Tatiana, I'm not sure about your sword or mine, but I know we still have some diamonds left. Let's make a new sword for you. I will use my old one. We need to go back and help our friends battle those evil griefers." Steve paced and ate food as he spoke.

"It's almost night," remarked Max. "I think we should stay here and help the villagers fight the skeletons."

"After watching that parade of skeletons, I bet the battle is going to be intense tonight," added Tatiana.

They walked to Georgia's crafting table. Tatiana and Max took two diamonds from their inventory and crafted swords and enchanted them at the enchantment table.

Bones rattled past the window. "They're here!" shouted Tatiana.

Georgia, Lucy, and Henry ran down the stairs. "We were defeated by the rainbow griefers; we want to help you battle the skeletons."

They used their remaining diamonds to craft new swords. As they crafted them, Lucy said, "The griefers trapped the others—after we defeat these skeletons we have to save them!"

Suited up in armor, the gang hurried through the streets of Georgia's village. Steve held a block of TNT and used flint and steel to ignite it. They destroyed a group of skeletons that were shooting arrows at the group.

The skeleton army that marched toward the town had finally arrived.

"How are we going to stop them?" Lucy said in a panic. "There are just way too many of them to even begin to battle."

"I have a plan!" Steve shouted as he took shelter from the flurry of arrows that were flying in their direction.

"What?" asked Max.

Before he could answer, Kyra, Olive, Sophie, and Nia raced toward them. They each carried a block of TNT and ignited it.

KABOOM!

The massive explosion wiped out a large portion of the army, but there were still over fifty skeletons left to battle.

"I thought you guys were trapped?" asked Max.

"We escaped," said Nia proudly.

"If you call being destroyed by a creeper escaping, then we escaped," added Olive.

The gang were gathering more TNT while Steve and Max struck skeletons with arrows, when Liam and Dylan sprinted toward them.

Steve hit Dylan with his diamond sword.

Dylan pleaded, "Please, we came back here to help you."

Liam begged, "We will fight the skeletons with you. Just help us."

"We don't have time to battle each other. We need to fight the skeletons," Steve said as he struck two skeletons.

A skeleton looked at Steve. It was the second time he felt that the skeletons were the ones who needed help. Maybe they were coming to the village as an escape from having to attack.

A sea of arrows flew past Lucy's head. "Steve," she called out, "didn't you say you had a plan?"

"Yes, but I'm not sure how it will work," confessed Steve.

"At this moment, any plan is a good one," replied Lucy.

A creeper walked past Steve.

"Watch out!" warned Max.

Kaboom! The creeper exploded, destroying Steve.

Steve awoke in his bed at Georgia's house. *I feel like this has happened before*, Steve joked to himself.

Steve walked to Georgia's kitchen and helped himself to a baked potato. The house was quiet. He wanted to go help his friends battle the skeletons, but the sun was rising and he knew it was more important to fill up his energy and food bars so he could prepare for his grand plan.

The sun began to rise. The skeletons disappeared and the group returned to Georgia's house. One by one they entered Georgia's living room, exhausted and in search of food.

"We destroyed Liam and Dylan!" Lucy boasted.

"I wonder if they will actually respawn in the prison they told us about or if that was just another one of their lies," Max said as he took a bite from a baked potato.

"I don't know where they'll respawn, but I'm glad they're gone. They are awful," said Tatiana.

Lucy announced to the group, "Steve has a plan."

"Yes, I do," replied Steve. "There were two times, when I was battling the skeletons, where I met eyes with the bony creatures and felt as if they were asking for help not to harm us."

"Really?" Henry was shocked. "They show up in this village and shoot arrows at everyone. They seem to enjoy destroying us."

"They are only trying to defend themselves," remarked Steve.

"What is your plan?" Lucy was beginning to think Steve's plan wasn't going to save them. She worried this was a never-ending battle and she wanted it to be over. The Overworld was filled with treasure, and she could be hunting it instead of spending her days in a village being attacked by skeletons.

"My plan is getting control of the skeleton army and getting them to attack the rainbow griefers instead of the villagers," announced Steve.

"That's a great plan!" exclaimed Lucy.

"Yeah, but how are you going to do that?" asked Henry.

15
THE GREAT ESCAPE

Steve paced the length of the quartz floor in Georgia's enormous living room. "This is how we'll do it. When the skeletons approach the village, we will run in the direction of the jungle. They will follow us and we'll hide."

"And?" questioned Lucy.

"Once we get there, I assume the rainbow griefers will attack. While the skeletons battle the rainbow griefers, we'll go down and destroy the skeleton farm. The skeletons will be so happy the farm is destroyed, they won't attack the village anymore." Steve was proud of his plan.

Steve's friends had many questions.

"How do you know the rainbow griefers will attack?" asked Georgia.

"Why do you think the skeletons will stop attacking when the spawner is destroyed?" questioned Sophie.

"Do you really think the skeletons will follow us back to the jungle?" Tatiana said skeptically.

"Does anybody have a better plan?" Steve defensively asked.

There was silence. Nobody had any other ideas.

"When night falls, we will see if my plan works. If it doesn't, then we are back to where we started. But we have to try," Steve instructed the group.

"Let's make some new armor," Sophie suggested, as the group worked on powerful weapons and armor for their battle. Suddenly they heard voices at the door.

"Who could that be?" Georgia rushed to the window and Lucy followed.

"Oh no!" Lucy screamed out. "It's Liam and Dylan!"

"Don't open it!" shouted Henry.

Georgia took out her diamond sword and opened the door. Pointing the sword at Liam and Dylan, she demanded, "What do you want?"

"We need your help," Liam cried.

"I thought you guys respawned in a prison. How did you get out?" questioned Steve.

"We want to return your stuff." Liam took out a bunch of diamond swords from his inventory and placed them in a chest.

"Please take this chest as a peace offering," said Dylan, and he placed the chest in Georgia's doorway.

"Why are you being so nice?" questioned Lucy.

"How did you get out of the prison?" Max wanted answers.

"We're not going to lie to you." Dylan stood by the chest and confessed, "We were griefers."

Liam interrupted him with "We *are* griefers."

Dylan clarified, "But we're not rainbow griefers."

"The rainbow griefers found us in the jungle and tried to recruit us to join their team," Liam said breathlessly.

"They demanded we change our skins and become rainbow griefers." Dylan spoke quickly and was visibly upset.

"We told them we didn't want to join them and they threatened us. We tried to escape but they trapped us in a prison. We were stuck there until you guys came along," said Liam.

"The rainbow griefers needed someone that wasn't rainbow to trick you guys. They seem to think you guys are hard to battle and they were worried when they saw you approach the village," Dylan stated and smiled.

"So we thought if the rainbow griefers are afraid of you, you can help us escape." Liam was hopeful.

"But every time we see you, you guys attack us." Tatiana was confused and angry.

"We only attack you when the rainbow griefers are there, because we don't want them to see us befriending you. We don't want them to think we've changed our minds and will join your team," explained Liam.

"You were mean to me when there were no rainbow griefers in sight," Steve told them, "and you teased me about my sword, when you were guarding the temple."

"And you trapped us in a bedrock box," added Sophie.

"We can explain!" Liam shouted above the others. "We were being watched by the rainbow griefers then. We escaped just now. There are no rainbow griefers here."

"Did you steal diamonds from my chest?" asked Georgia. "We had a chest filled with diamonds and now they're gone."

Liam and Dylan didn't want to lie anymore. Dylan tearfully confessed, "Yes, we did. The rainbow griefers demanded that we get the treasure you had stolen from the temple. They were infuriated that you got away with their treasure, so we were instructed to steal it."

"We can't get it back. The rainbow griefers have it and I don't know where they're hiding it," said Liam.

"How can we know you're telling the truth?" asked Steve.

Liam and Dylan walked into Georgia's living room and placed their diamond swords on the ground.

"Now we have no weapons. If you strike us, we'll be destroyed," said Liam.

"My health bar is so low," added Dylan, "one strike from any of you and I'll be gone."

"I can't do this anymore. I just want to go home to my village," Liam said weakly.

"We all feel the same way. We want to go home. We're going to trust you. But when we see the rainbow griefers, you have to fight *with* us, not against us," Steve told the two tricksters.

The gang was very upset with Steve's decision. They protested.

"I'm sorry, Steve. I'm not helping them," Max said angrily.

Sophie wondered if Steve had the right idea and they should give the two griefers a chance. If they were going to attempt to execute Steve's plan, they'd need all the help they could get. "Maybe Steve is right. We should let them join us."

"Maybe Steve is wrong!" countered Nia.

"This could be a trap. I don't trust them," exclaimed Olive.

"We didn't agree to this! I don't trust these guys," Georgia shouted.

Click! Clack! Clang!

The evening attack had begun.

"We have no time to discuss this. We'll just have to see what happens," Steve announced as he rushed out of Georgia's house and led the army of skeletons toward the lush green jungle, back to the temple where they had been spawned.

The others followed closely behind. Everyone had a different opinion about Liam and Dylan, but they all had the same goal. They wanted to stop the skeleton attacks on the village and they needed to destroy the spawner. And they wanted to destroy the rainbow griefers.

They sprinted toward the village. Dylan and Liam followed. Steve could make out an army of rainbow griefers in the distance. This was the moment Dylan and Liam had to prove they were on Steve and his friends' side. This was the moment Steve would realize if he had made the right decision.

16
ALLY OR ENEMY?

"**H**ide!" Steve shouted to his friends. The group took shelter behind a large tree.

The skeletons continued toward the temple.

"Do you think that's all of the skeletons?" asked Lucy, "or are any in town? And are they attacking the town?"

Nia replied, "I didn't follow you guys until I saw the last skeleton leave the village."

The skeletons shot arrows at the rainbow griefers.

"I think your plan is working, Steve!" exclaimed Lucy.

The rainbow griefers' diamond swords were no match for the skeleton army.

Steve looked over at Liam and Dylan as the two griefers gleefully watched the skeleton army obliterating the rainbow griefers.

"Look, they're getting destroyed by their own creation," noted Nia.

"We can't sit here anymore. We need to go in and deactivate that spawner!" Steve told the gang.

As the remaining rainbow griefers struggled to battle the enormous bony beasts, the gang snuck into the temple.

"We need to head down here," Liam said and he led the way. "I know how they are working this skeleton farm."

Against their better instincts, the group followed Liam downstairs.

"This better not be a trap!" warned Lucy.

"It's not!" Liam defended himself.

The spawner was on and creating bony mobs. Skeletons appeared in the cage and were led straight to the kill room.

"I don't get it. How are they escaping?" questioned Georgia.

Steve inspected the spawner, noticing a small hole. He watched as the skeletons climbed out of the hole and up the stairs.

"I bet the rainbow griefers don't even want these skeletons to attack the village. They just don't know their spawner is broken." Steve grabbed two blocks of TNT and used flint and steel to destroy the spawner.

Kaboom!

The group shielded themselves from the blast. The noise from the explosion alerted the rainbow griefers to the gang's location. Within seconds a horde of rainbow griefers sprinted down the stairs, ready to attack Steve and his friends.

Liam and Dylan were the first to confront the rainbow griefers. Liam struck one of the griefers with his diamond sword. Dylan shot an arrow at the other one.

Steve battled the rainbow griefers alongside Liam and Dylan, but paused when a creeper crept up near the two reformed griefers.

"Watch out!" Steve warned them, but the creeper exploded, destroying Liam, Dylan, and the rainbow griefers they were battling.

With clashing swords and flying arrows, the gang and the rainbow griefers were in an intense battle.

"Look who joined the fight!" screamed Steve. The rainbow griefers turned to see a gang of skeletons come down the stairs while shooting arrows at the griefers.

One of the skeletons looked over and noticed the spawner had been destroyed. The skeleton looked over at Steve. Steve could swear he smiled, but he knew hostile mobs never showed any signs of emotion.

The last rainbow griefer looked at Steve. "Why?" he asked him.

"This was your battle. You started all of this," Steve told the griefer. "When you create evil skeleton farms, sometimes it can backfire on you. Sometimes you can get destroyed by your own weapons."

Max sprinted toward the remaining rainbow griefer, hitting him with a final blow that destroyed the griefer.

There was an eerie calm. Then the gang heard voices crying for help.

"Who is that?" questioned Olive.

"Help us!" the voices begged.

"I think it's Liam and Dylan and they're trapped," Steve said as he walked in the direction of the voices.

"I believe they're coming from underneath us," said Lucy.

The group took out their pickaxes and dug a hole in the ground.

"Watch out!" screamed Lucy as a creeper made its way toward them.

Max shot an arrow at the creeper and it exploded.

Kaboom! The blast left a big hole in the ground.

Henry looked down to the lower level. "I think I see a bedrock door."

"How are we going to break into a bedrock prison?" asked Steve. "I don't have the cube of destruction."

"I don't have very much energy left," Lucy admitted, because she was exhausted.

Everyone was running low on energy. Georgia said, "We have to head back to my house and replenish our energy. We need to eat and rest."

"We can't leave Liam and Dylan," Steve told the group. "They proved they were on our side when they joined us in battle. We have to save them, even if it takes our last bit of energy."

The group stood there silently.

"If you don't want to help me, I'll do it alone," Steve declared. "I will break down that bedrock wall and free them from the rainbow griefers."

"But what if the rainbow griefers come back?" asked Sophie.

"What if this is another trap?" questioned Tatiana.

"What if it isn't and we left two people trapped in a prison? I couldn't live with myself if I stopped caring about other people," replied Steve.

"But they bullied you and stole your sword," said Henry.

"They apologized and gave the sword back to me." And with that comment Steve jumped through the hole in the ground and jogged toward the bedrock wall.

"Help!" The voices grew louder.

"Don't worry," said Steve, "I'm going to get you out of here."

"Steve!" Liam and Dylan called out. "Please help us!"

Steve looked at the wall, hoping there was a small hole he could use to get them out, but there was nothing. He dug his pickaxe into the ground. He would mine a hole into the center of the room.

Steve looked at his hunger bar. He wasn't sure he'd have enough energy to complete the hole, but he had to try. As he stood alone in the basement of the temple, he tried to help his new friends escape. *It was a hard job,* Steve told himself, *but it wasn't impossible.*

Steve looked up and saw all of his friends standing in front of him. Each of them carried a pickaxe and helped Steve dig the hole in the ground.

"You don't have to do this alone," Max said as he smiled at Steve.

"Maybe we're not Liam and Dylan's biggest fans, but you were the one who had the plan that saved my village.

You're my friend and I have to help you," Georgia said as she dug her pickaxe deep into the ground.

"We have to do this fast!" Henry announced. "We're all running out of energy."

Liam called to them, "Help! There are two spiders in here and we don't have any weapons!"

17
RACE AGAINST TIME

The group dug as fast at they could. Dylan and Liam's cries grew louder.

"We're cornered by the spider!" they shouted.

Steve crawled through the hole, emerging in the center of the prison. He took out his diamond sword and struck the spider.

Max and Henry poked their heads through the hole and jumped in to destroy the remaining spider.

"You're free!" Steve announced to Liam and Dylan.

"Steve, we have to repay you. You saved our lives," Dylan said as he followed Steve and the gang through the hole and out of the prison.

Liam was overjoyed. "Now we can go back to our village."

"Are you still going to be griefers?" Steve asked both of them when they were safely outside the temple. The sun was beating down and there was a calm quiet throughout the jungle.

"I don't know," admitted Liam, "but I can promise we won't attack you."

"We are going back to my village to help rebuild. Do you want to join us?" asked Georgia.

"That's a nice offer," said Dylan, "but we need to head home."

The group parted ways with Liam and Dylan and headed back to the village.

"I guess you were right, Steve," remarked Henry. "They weren't planning on tricking us."

As they made their way back to the village, rain started to pour down on them. A skeleton jumped out at them from behind a tree, shooting an arrow at the group.

"Oh no!" cried Lucy.

Max lunged at the bony menace with his diamond sword.

"Where are the others?" Georgia looked around to see an empty rainy jungle.

"I guess that was one of the last skeletons," remarked Steve.

"Or maybe it was simply a naturally occurring hostile mob and the world has returned to normal," added Sophie.

"This means I can finally stop carrying around blocks of TNT," declared Nia, who was happy to stop battling the hostile mobs.

The rain cleared as they approached Georgia's village.

"I'm home!" she called out. "Let's go help people rebuild."

The townspeople came out of their homes and thanked Steve and his friends. They threw a feast for the group, and the gang devoured all the goodies. They needed to get their strength back. The atmosphere was jovial. The town was ready to rebuild and was excited for their first evening without a skeleton attack.

Evening set in and there were no skeletons to be seen. Steve and the gang walked back to Georgia's house to get some sleep. Two Endermen carrying blocks walked past the group. Although they knew not to stare at this lanky mob, one of the Endermen shrieked and began to teleport toward Olive.

"Help!" she cried to the group.

The group went to attack the Enderman, but then drops of rain poured from the sky. Thunder boomed, as the gang made their way to the safety of Georgia's house.

They bolted through the door and raced to their beds. Exhausted, they all fell asleep, restoring their energy for the next day. They were going to help the village rebuild everything that was destroyed in the attacks, especially Georgia's farm.

As Steve lay in his bed, he thought about the fence he was building at home and how he had thought that was such an important project. After dealing with the skeleton attacks and the amount of rebuilding Georgia's town needed, he knew the fence was a minor task in comparison.

Although he felt bad for the townspeople and all of their property that was destroyed in the attacks, he was excited to rebuild. He had so many ideas. But for now, he had to concentrate on falling asleep.

18

REBUILD AND RELOCATE

Georgia offered her guests cake for breakfast. "We need to start out our day celebrating!" she told the group as they devoured the cake. "Today is the day we start to rebuild."

The gang walked into the town. Olive asked Steve if he could help rebuild her house. "I've been living with Nia. My house was destroyed. Georgia told me you were one of the best builders she has ever seen."

"I think Georgia is a better builder than I am, but I'd love to help you." Steve walked to the plot where Olive's house once stood.

Steve walked around the land surrounding the home. He could see the jungle in the distance. "Why don't we make a large house with a picture window, so you can have a view of the jungle in the distance?" he suggested.

"Yes, so I can be the first to see if we are ever attacked again," replied Olive as she helped Steve gather all the supplies to build a new home.

Lucy, Max, and Henry approached Steve. Henry said, "I think we're going to go on a treasure hunt. Georgia told me there is a desert not far from here. We want to find a desert temple and get some treasure."

"We'll stay and help build for a few days," added Lucy, "but after we're done we want to go exploring, not back to the wheat farm."

Steve was sad that he wouldn't be heading back to the wheat farm with his friends, but he knew they wanted to hunt for treasure. Kyra walked toward Steve.

"Did they tell you their plans?" asked Kyra.

"Are you going treasure hunting with them?" Steve asked Kyra.

"No, I'm going back home with you, and so are Tatiana and Sophie. They want to reunite with Eliot the Blacksmith and settle in our village."

Steve was still disappointed that his friends Lucy, Max, and Henry weren't traveling back with him, but he was excited to have his new friends Tatiana and Sophie settle in his town.

Tatiana and Sophie raced toward Steve. "We're going to be neighbors," said Tatiana.

"Can you help us build a new home?" asked Sophie.

Steve was going to do a lot of building in the next few months. "Can you help me repair my fence?" asked Steve.

"Of course," replied Tatiana, "that's what friends are for. We can't wait to help you."

The whole gang helped Olive construct a new home. It wasn't as lavish as Georgia's house, but it had a quartz floor and a fireplace. It also had a picture window that looked out at the jungle.

"I don't know how to thank you," exclaimed Olive.

The group was sad to leave the town. Lucy, Max, and Henry suited up and headed toward the desert in search of treasure, while Tatiana and Sophie joined Steve and Kyra on their journey back to the wheat farm.

Georgia said good-bye to her friends. "Please come and visit." Olive and Nia also invited everyone back.

"Next time you're around this village, let us know and we'll plan another feast," said Olive.

Steve looked out at Georgia's village. It was peaceful and flourishing. Everyone's home had been rebuilt. Steve smiled at Georgia. Everyone promised to return one day as they set out on their own separate journeys. Steve was excited for the moment when he reached his village. He imagined walking into Eliot's blacksmith shop. His heart skipped a beat when he pictured surprising his friend Eliot with these two people from his old village.

Tatiana and Sophie were finally going to have a new home, and Steve would have more neighbors. He had help for rebuilding his wheat farm and friends with which to share his crops.

The End

DO YOU LIKE FICTION FOR MINECRAFTERS?

Check out other unofficial Minecrafter adventures from Sky Pony Press!

Invasion of the Overworld

MARK CHEVERTON

Battle for the Nether

MARK CHEVERTON

Confronting the Dragon

MARK CHEVERTON

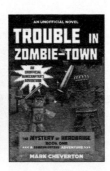

Trouble in Zombie-town

MARK CHEVERTON

The Quest for the Diamond Sword

WINTER MORGAN

The Mystery of the Griefer's Mark

WINTER MORGAN

The Endermen Invasion

WINTER MORGAN

Treasure Hunters in Trouble

WINTER MORGAN

Available wherever books are sold!